NO SURPRISES

100 FLASH FICTION STORIES

ANDREA C. NEIL

No Surprises, 100 Flash Fiction Stories

Paperback ISBN 978-1-7334154-7-7

This is a work of fiction. Names, characters, places, and incidents either are the products of the author's imagination or are used fictitiously. Any resemblance to actual persons, living or dead, businesses, companies, events, or locales is entirely coincidental.

Published by 1631 Press, LLC

INTRODUCTION

In June of 2022, I packed my suitcase for a three-week vacation in Southern California, and at the end of September, I finally made it home. Some years, that's just how things go.

I went out to visit my dad, who was on hospice but still quite chipper. By the end of the three weeks, however, intuition politely suggested I stay longer. I'd like to say I didn't know what I was getting myself into, but that's not really true. I knew I was staying to see him through the last stages of his life.

It's funny, those times in my life when time seems to go so slowly that I want to burst into tears with each new minute that is born. Then suddenly, I'm looking back at it all, at the blur of events that cascaded onto themselves over and over again. On some level it makes sense, even if I can't quite get it into words.

My summer was like that.

In July, I thought it would be a "fun experiment" to try writing a 100-word story every day, like I did back in 2020 (see *Days Are Beautiful,* my first collection of flash fiction.) I thought it might be a good way to mark time, deal with stress. I guess it was those things. But it ended up being so much more than that too.

On September 8, 2022 (story #48/100), my dad passed away, heading off into the unknown for a new adventure. It was an intense time—perhaps that's a story for another day—but I'm glad I was there, and I know things turned out how they were supposed to turn out. As my dad used to like to say, "One cannot escape one's destiny." Ha-effing-ha, Dad.

I hope that as you read this book, you'll be entertained by the weird and funny and sometimes sad stories that I wrote from July through November. I didn't quite make my one-per-day quota. So sue me.

Maybe they'll resonate with you on some meaningful level. Maybe you'll just like the one about the sharks. In the end, it's just entertainment!

But if we don't move through all these things, if we don't take all the feelings and gather them up and hold them in our hearts, how will we ever learn?

Here's to our eternal education.

Andrea C. Neil

December 2022

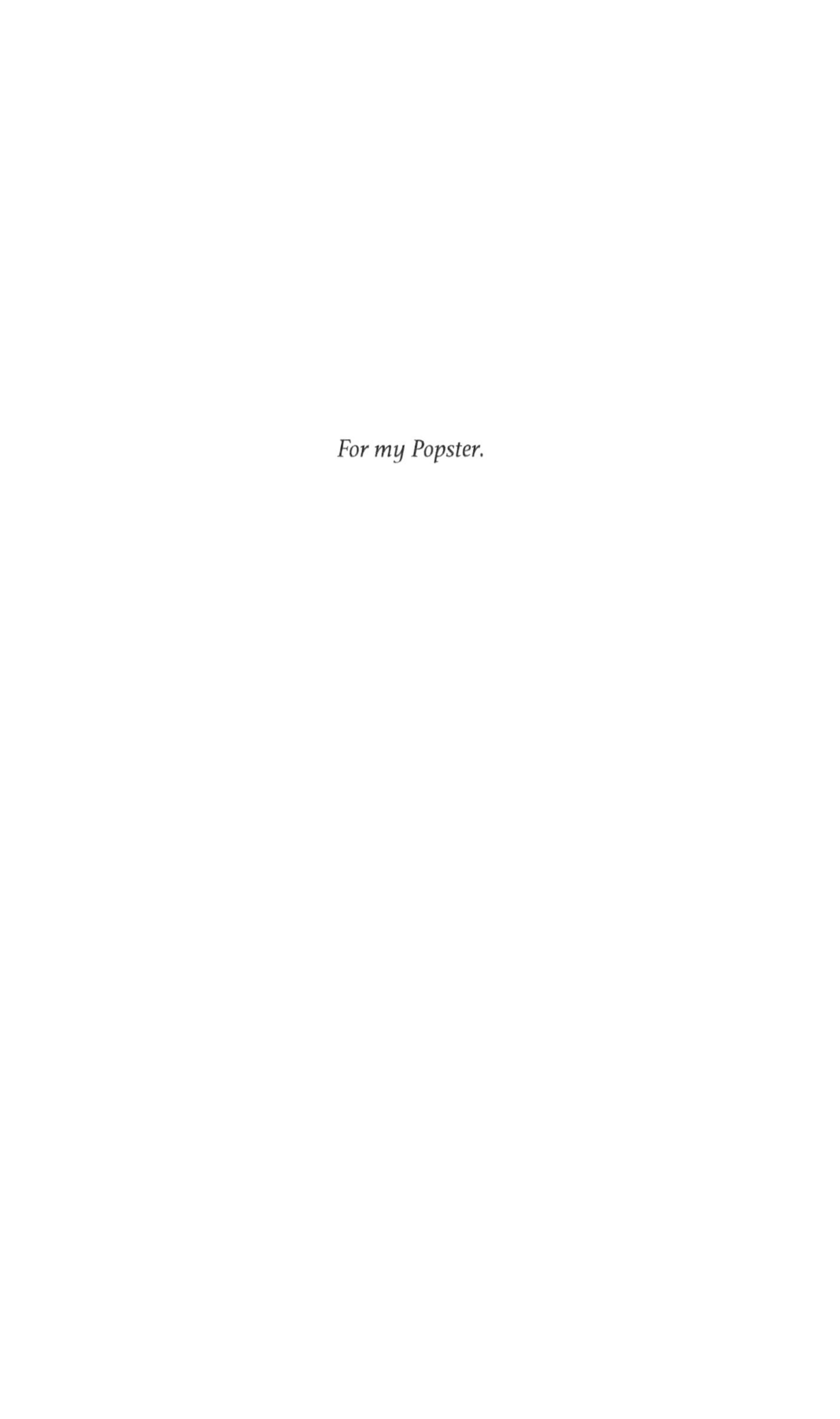

For my Popster.

The Mountain

Each day, she climbed as high as she could before her legs would give out. She never knew that her lungs could feel like they would implode and explode at the same time until she had started the ascent, thirty-nine days earlier.

Up and up and up. She couldn't see the top, only what was below, where she had already been. But still she knew the top was there somewhere. It had to be. If it wasn't, this would all have been for nothing—the climbing, the pain, the not knowing. Surely the top was up there somewhere.

Thirsty Bird

I needed shade so I walked around the side of the house and sat on the front steps under a pine tree. The air was so dry. It felt like the pine needles under my feet might catch fire. When I looked up, there was Crow. Beak open, hopping from branch to branch.

"What's new?" I asked.

"Hot," he said. "No water."

I looked down at my feet. "I know. Sorry."

"Why do you apologize for something that's not your fault?" Crow asked, landing on the ground.

"Everything's my fault," I said.

He thought for a moment. "Okay."

Spirited Feet

Lucy awoke from a nap on her yoga mat, deciding it counted as her daily practice. Before rising, she stuck her feet in the air. Suddenly harp music began to play, and her toes glowed.

"What the—" she exclaimed.

"Don't curse," said a soft female voice.

"For Christ's sake," said a crisp male voice, "let her do whatever the fuck she wants."

"Who are you?" asked Lucy.

"We're your feet angels," said the female.

"Feet ... angels?"

"Yeah," said the male, irritated. "You know, *feet angels*."

"My dear," said the female, "every step you take is holy."

Comme Ce

The server stood tableside, steepling his fingers in anticipatory glee. "Oh yes, oui, but of course."

"Good," said Bart. Not every restaurant could accommodate his unusual culinary requests, but he had hope that finally, here by the sea in Monaco, he had found The Place.

Bart's date looked down at her cleavage, sighed, and adjusted the 2-inch-wide straps that doubled as the front of her evening dress. He caught the waiter stealing a glance.

"Whatever it costs," said Bart.

The server bowed and left the table without a word.

This was going to be good, in every language.

Real Life

"Mom, where did Ranger go when Dad said he bought the farm?"

"Is that what he told you? I swear, that man."

"Right, but where did Ranger go? Did he really buy a farm? What's he growing?"

"Well sure, he bought a farm. He won the doggie lottery and bought some land where he could grow and raise his favorite things."

"Like peanut butter? And cat poop?"

"Yes dear, just like that."

"Is that where Gampy went? Did he win the lottery and buy a farm?"

"Uh-huh."

"Can we visit?"

"At some point, my darling, at some point."

Good Will

Autumnleaf held a blouse to Moonforest's chest. "This is sooo perfect for you."

Moonforest looked down. "I know, right? Like, totally."

"It's totally you—on Sunset, with an updo and your Docs."

"Nice."

They continued browsing, and talked over the heads of other shoppers.

"So where are you like, working now?" asked Moonforest.

"I do the onboarding for this agency in WeHo. It's like, totally different work for me." Autumnleaf pulled a dress off the rack. "Oh my god! This is soooo authentically '90s!" She looked at it closer. "Actually it might be a little too authentically '90s."

Fish Stories

Grant used his left pectoral fin to clock in for his shift. He nodded hello to Marty, and they began the twenty-minute swim toward shore.

"What's cookin'?" asked Marty.

No answer.

"You not talkin' again today?"

After still getting no reply, Marty shrugged, and they swam in silence. Soon the fins of surfboards could be seen above, along with a few submerged legs sporting tasty-looking calves.

"Don't you ever just wonder what it's all for?" asked Grant. "I mean, is there a purpose to all this?"

This time Marty was speechless.

"Never mind. Let's get it over with."

Hot Day

Inland was stifling, so Durga went to the beach. She took Crow for company since Shiva was golfing.

Once there, Crow flew off to visit a group of kin by the trash cans to catch up. Durga got comfortable in her chair.

The beach always sounded like a good idea, but in truth it was boring. When you've read every book in existence and didn't need a smartphone, distractions were limited.

Several young female surfers caught her eye. Their hair was dripping wet, and they laughed as they carried their boards with ease. Ah, to be young again.

Exciting Opportunity

AVAILABLE NOW!

Got some waiting around to do but don't want to bother? Your troubles are over!

No job too large or small. We assist with everything from checkout lines to that heavy yet inevitable existential other shoe.

Plumber running late? We'll let them in.

DoorDash hasn't shown with your Chipotle? We'll watch the app.

Feeling like you're just killing time on the planet? We can help with that.*

Whatever your waiting needs are, we're standing by.

Life is short, so don't waste any of it! Let us do it.

·   ·   ·

*Surcharge for long-term waits requiring professional counseling experience

Harrison's Nose

"What's this button?"

Without waiting, I pushed it. *BWOOP!* The spacecraft wobbled and the hangar around us got really huge, really fast.

"Mr. Ford isn't on board yet!" the captain admonished me.

The airborne ship approached a large object which looked like a moon-sized wool blue blazer. A deep, deafening noise erupted from the giant blazer and the spaceship was sucked upward.

"He's gonna blow! You idiot!" That part was directed at me again.

And that was the last time we were ever seen—after Harrison Ford's sneeze blew our tiny spaceship onto the wind and into oblivion.

Fat Chance

Dougie was obsessed with whipped cream. He ate it on absolutely anything. A nice glass of ice water was better with a dollop of the fluffy topping. Pancakes, sushi, avocado—it was all fair game.

The spray stuff in the can was okay in a pinch, easy enough to dispense at a moment's notice. But Dougie's favorite whipped cream was what he made by hand, from the full-fat cream of cows raised in southern France.

He achieved fame for making the best whipped cream in the world, became a chef, and retired when his YouTube channel took off.

Deep Thoughts

Mercy thought a lot about what it would be like to be part of nature. Not just being in nature, but really of it.

What would it be like to be a tree? Would she want to be a fruit tree, bearing delicious gifts, or a tall redwood, living for hundreds of years?

Some days she thought it'd be nice to be an animal, like a fox or bear. Spider, not so much.

Finally, she decided that if she were to be of nature, she'd be a rock on the bottom of the sea. Yes, that'd be good.

Thin Air

"It's hard to breathe up here," I said to Crow.

Crow stayed silent, hopping from foot to foot in the snow, beak open.

I sat on a rock to eat a snack before continuing up the side of the mountain. The terrain had gotten steeper as the morning went on. More slippery. Icy.

How could I get much farther? My lungs weren't used to the altitude. I wasn't dressed right for the cold, and as I looked up, I still couldn't see the summit.

And what was I here for? What was the purpose?

I couldn't remember anymore.

Gimmee Coffee

The "aha" moment—this is good!

V60 pourover using a gooseneck kettle. Hario scale. Hand ground. Store ground. Capresso grinder. Latte. Iced. Cold brew. Espresso, cappuccino, steamed milk. Cow's milk. With lots of milk. Almond milk. Soy milk. Oat milk. No milk.

Brazilian, Costa Rican, Guatamalan, Ethiopian, Honduran, Colombian, Kenyan. Decaf, half caff. Full caff. Instant.

Coffee adventures on vacation.

Mind-blowingly delicious, mediocre. Shitty. Embarrassingly shitty. Overindulgence. Tapering off. Once a day. Twice per day. Cold turkey.

Flavor profiles. Tastings. Mouthfeel. Brewing temperature.

What will I remember about it all when I'm old?

"I used to drink coffee."

Desert Pool

Ellory "Ellie" McFinn was on a posh summer desert holiday. She'd rented the fanciest house with the nicest pool. She did her best thinking by the pool, so she couldn't do without.

As it so happened, a friend was staying nearby, Miss Lesta Runningdeer. Lesta had been vacationing with her lover, Franklin Whitmore ... until Frank turned up dead, shoved into the pantry with a bread roll stuffed in his mouth.

Ellie called her favorite police detective, Jack Robinson, to join her at her residence—there was plenty of room. And besides, they had a murder to solve.

Sea Ya

There once was a sea snake 1,000 miles long and half a mile wide. It writhed with such force when swimming that Hawaii experienced high surf when it rounded the Cape of Good Hope.

The sea snake decided it wanted a friend. Up north it spotted a beautiful creature lurking in the shallow waters off Iceland. The creature was almost as big as it was, and thinking it had found a kindred spirit, the sea snake approached.

Unfortunately, the creature wasn't benevolent and became enraged at being disturbed. Alas, we lost the last giant sea snake in existence.

Cold Treat

Durga watched the trio of girls perched on the stone bench, eating frozen yogurt. She wasn't sure why she was so preoccupied with youth and the trappings thereof. But she did know it was a phase, just like everything else in her infinite existence—sooner or later she'd be back around to thinking about death all the time.

But really, wasn't thinking about youth the same as thinking about death? Two sides of the same coin, as someone said once.

Or in her case, two flowers in the garden of the universe, to be admired but never picked.

Curious Curio

Stella found herself once again in the little shop filled with candles, books, and bits and bobs that looked inconsequential until you got up close and realized they were of some import. Everywhere she looked, stuff.

As she rounded a corner display of dried rabbit poop (the placard said it was good for loneliness but didn't say what you were supposed to do with it), she heard her name being called.

"Stella…"

It seemed to be coming from a book on the top shelf of the back wall.

"Stella. Yo, Stella."

The book's title was *Lost Dreams.*

Sweet Desert

Detective Jack Robinson arrived at Ellie's desert oasis by taxi, suitcase in one hand and hat in the other. After admonishing himself for being at her beck and call, he rang the bell and was told to go directly to the pool.

And there she was. A stunning vision in the unbearable heat.

"Hello Jack," she said, lowering her sunglasses to look him over. "Have a drink."

He sat, took off his coat, and pulled deeply from whatever iced concoction he'd been handed.

"Shouldn't we be off to see Lesta?" he asked.

"Give it a minute," she said.

Who Knows

Beatrice looked at the alarm clock—6:30 a.m.! The start of another brand-new day! What heavenly miracles would befall her? What good fortune lay on the other side of a delicious breakfast? The only way to know for sure was to get out of bed and see.

Her avocado toast was perfect. The sourdough bread was fragrant and springy, the avocado seasoned just right. She'd never had a riper peach in her life! It was as if nature blossomed on her tongue. It was a marvelous morning.

Then she took out her phone and ruined the whole day.

Great Heights

She'd been climbing for what felt like forever. Her tears turned to salty ice on her cheeks and Crow had given up, preferring to stay tucked in her bag instead of flying.

One evening, she spotted a small building with stone walls, built to withstand the weather. A light through a small window beckoned her. Surely they'd not mind a visitor?

She knocked and opened the door to a small room with a blazing fire in the corner and a woman sitting in a chair wearing the most resplendent silks she'd ever seen.

"Right on time," Durga said.

Right Side

She played the three-second clip over and over again. Watched every single nuance of movement. His left hand in the bottom right corner of the frame.

The man sat on a stool, instrument held in his right hand, left hand spread across the top of his thigh. Then, with one quick movement, he brushed his fingers across his jeans before standing up and leaving the stage.

In those seconds she observed the shape of his fingers, their grace and elegance. That one simple movement done without thought, with innocence.

All her heart wished for a love like that.

The Rules

"You're playin' with that damn thing all wrong."

"Nuh-uh, Pop-pop. You put the cars at the top and watch them race to the bottom!" Junior pointed to the finish line.

"Yeah, right." Pop-pop was still sprightly for his age, so he knelt by the plastic racetrack and put three cars at the finish line, facing uphill. "You start out at the bottom. If you're lucky, you bust your ass and get partway up that hill. Maybe you get to the top but even if you do, someone pushes you off the edge."

Junior frowned.

"Just being realistic, kiddo."

Everybody (P)Oops

Elephants do. Mice, rats, moles, chipmunks, and squirrels. Whales, ferrets, sloths, as well as night herons.

Bears and bunnies!

The domesticated beasts for sure—cats and dogs, hamsters, guinea pigs, parakeets, goldfish. Horses, oxen, cows, donkeys. Chickens, ducks, pigs, sheep.

All the rest of the quadrupeds.

Even fierce cougars and jaguars.

Snakes, lizards, iguanas, turtles. All reptiles, in fact. Toads. Newts. Salamanders. Slimy things.

Millipedes! Centipedes and the boring-by-comparison eight-legged spiders.

All the teeny tiny things, like amoebas, plankton (the zooplankton, the holoplankton *and* the meroplankton). Krill, water fleas.

Sharks, stingrays, playful dolphins.

And humans.

Everyone makes mistakes.

Dear Sheila

The old man climbed the steps to his bedroom, huffing at the top. Those stairs were getting harder to navigate, he observed.

He turned on his bedside lamp. It was in the shape of a small turtle, the shell emitting a soft, yellow light that was comforting. Like he wasn't alone. The turtle kept him company through the darkness of the night.

The man had named the turtle lamp Sheila, and he admired her from his recliner. Just him and Sheila. It was how he wanted it. He closed his eyes and the two of them drifted off.

Baked Mystery

Ellie McFinn and Detective Jack Robinson walked to Lesta Runningdeer's house in the boiling midday heat. The local police had already removed the body of Mr. Franklin Whitmore from the pantry where it'd been found. The bread roll which had been unceremoniously stuffed in his mouth by the killer lay on the kitchen counter.

"Why am I here if local law enforcement is on the case?" asked Jack, noticing a bite had been taken from the roll.

Ellie shot him a look like he was being ridiculous. "You're being ridiculous," she said. "I want the best for Lesta."

Hot Flash

Instead of walking through the living room, Renata stopped and sat on the couch. Which became problematic when she realized she couldn't bring herself to get off it.

In slow motion, her torso leaned to the left and she landed on her side, the lower half of her body still in a sitting position.

Had she entered into another dimension? An alternate reality? A month ago, her life had gotten intense. A week ago, things had gotten more intense, making last month seem inconsequential. Today, things were so intense she wasn't sure how much more she could handle.

Aggro Curtains

Bert was mad. Hopping mad. Seeing red.

Everything set him off. His mom made his favorite cookies, but he refused to eat them. His best friend came to play but Bert sent her away. Even an invitation to go fishing with his dad was refused. Bert just sat in the living room and fumed.

"What is wrong with you?" his mom asked. She knew raising a boy was challenging, but this was too much.

Bert didn't answer his mom, just shrugged and crossed his arms.

His mom huffed. "Ever since we got these red curtains you've been impossible!"

Inscrutable Humor

Durga scrutinized the woman standing before her, warming herself by the fire. After eons of moving through time and space based on intuition, Durga wasn't surprised to find herself high in the mountains with someone having a hard time. But she was disappointed by the mediocre digs. Clearly she would need to give this girl some mojo so she could get herself into some better scenery.

"What is your biggest concern?" Durga asked.

The woman frowned. "Sometimes I don't know how to be human."

Durga emitted laughter that echoed through the valleys and made the howling wind quicken.

Move Forward

Cherise's footsteps made no sound as she walked her path. Muted browns and greens lined the way—dense, unforgiving foliage. If she tried to peer through the growth, she saw only darkness.

She tried to remember what she'd told her father all those years ago. Some optimistic crap about being able to change the colors, change the direction of the whole damn path. Now here she was, traveling a dark road. No rainbows or unicorns for her.

Suddenly the ground gave way to nothingness. A swirl of white light encircled her and when it closed, she was complete.

Hot Dog

"Goddammit, it's too hot to be outside."

Frank looked at Shelley, who sat panting in the shade. He felt sorry for her—she did look hot. "You'll get used to it," he said, thinking he was being helpful.

"I resent your tone, Frank," she snapped.

Frank sat too. It wasn't worth getting into it. Why was it so hard to get along? No matter what he tried, he couldn't find a way to communicate that was satisfactory to her. Which was a shame since they lived together. He rolled over on his back to look at the sky.

Hold Up

Waiting waiting waiting waiting waiting

Loving

Eating

Sleeping waking sleeping waking sleeping waking waking

Waiting

Working

Waiting waiting

Holding releasing holding releasing releasing releasing loving

Working

Texting calling

Watching seeing sensing feeling

Seeing

Hurting

Waiting waiting waiting waiting waiting waiting waiting

Preparing planning coalescing

Cooking eating making eating cooking

Bathing dressing

Offering giving allowing letting helping

Allowing

Leaving leaving

Coming going

Leaving

Waiting waiting waiting waiting waiting waiting waiting

Talking listening talking listening listening listening listening listening listening

Feeling laughing crying listening

Waiting

Holding holding

Waiting

Going coming going coming leaving

Waiting

Going

Witnessing

Breathing

Breathing

Breathing

Breath.

Bright Light

A string of polished sandalwood mala beads lay on the table.

"What're those for?" asked the child, pointing to the necklace.

"Those are for prayers, son," answered the mother. She ran her fingers along the small wooden orbs, remembering her own mother.

"They look like you could pretend each one is a spaceship!"

"Maybe each one *is* a spaceship!" she said.

The child's eyes grew wide, considering the possibilities. "That would be fun."

"Yes," said the mother. "One hundred and eight spaceships, orbiting around the sun."

She picked up the beautiful beads and placed them around his neck.

Cute Vermin

Vernon sat on a log nibbling an unripe fig he'd plucked from a nearby tree. "It's just not fair," he said. "We get a bad rap because we eat garbage and chew through wires and do unsanitary things where humans wish we wouldn't."

Allan was a few feet away, chewing through the stucco wall of someone's garage. He sighed. "I know. Don't they get it that we have feelings too?"

They heard the crunch of human footsteps. "Maybe this is our chance to change things," suggested Vernon.

Allan knew Vernon was deluding himself and didn't have a reply.

Simple Question

She felt better, now that her bones had stopped aching from the cold and the woman with fierce eyes dressed in brightly colored silks had offered her a cup of the most delicious hot tea. They sat with Crow by the fire.

"So what are we doing here?" asked the woman with fierce eyes.

"I don't know what I'm doing here. How would I know what *you're* doing here?"

"This is your story," said the fierce woman.

That made the other woman pause. She'd never thought of it that way.

Why had she been doing all this climbing?

Feminine Mystery

Detective Robinson sat with Ellie McFinn and Lesta Runningdeer by the pool of Ellie's desert holiday oasis. Lesta was a beautiful woman, but he only had eyes for Ellie.

"What do you make of the bread roll in Whitmore's mouth?" asked Ellie. She wore dark glasses, but her eyebrows were inquisitive and alluring.

"I just can't believe it," said Lesta.

Jack could believe it. "Were you and he..."

"Lovers?" asked Lesta. Jack blushed.

Ellie laughed. "God Jack, you're hilarious."

He feared this woman would torment him for the rest of his days. Would that be so bad?

More Yarns

I knit my friend Joseph a pair of socks because his feet were cold.

I knit my friend Beth a hat to keep her head toasty.

I knit my friend Liz a scarf to protect her throat.

I knit my friend Bruce a sweater to warm his heart.

I knit my friend Liam mittens so he could walk comfortably in the winter woods.

I knit my friend Tess a cowl to lend warmth to her voice.

I knit my friend Mandy a shawl to pull close when she needed a hug.

What did I knit for myself?

Friendship.

Three Trees

Once there were three trees who were siblings of sorts. Perhaps they'd been cuttings from a single parent. They were planted the perfect distance apart—not too close that they crowded each other, but close enough that they kept one another company. Just like a good family would do.

The trees grew together. They learned to brace against the same wind. They gasped the same dirty air and fought for water as one. They maintained their distance, but over the years grew more content with sharing their space.

If only people could be as peaceful as the trees.

Big Cheese

"I need Cheetos."

"No, I don't think you do."

"Who are you to say what I need?"

"I'm your mother. You don't need Cheetos."

"Yes, but maybe that's just your perception of reality—that you're my mother."

"It's also my perception of reality that you don't need Cheetos."

"But what is a Cheeto, exactly? Who's to say what they are and who can have one? Certainly not you, Doris."

"Stop calling me Doris, you're supposed to call me mom. And see those grapes?"

"Yes."

"Well, in this reality, they're Cheetos. You can have as many as you want."

So Tired

I'm so tired that following politics seems like a good idea. I'm so tired that I want to do aerial yoga. I'm so tired that it feels like my brain is continuously buffering. I'm so tired that one night of good sleep doesn't do jack. I'm so tired that I don't want to watch romcoms. I'm so tired that chocolate for dinner sounds like a viable option. I'm too tired to knit. I'm so tired that this is the best I could come up with for a 100-word story. But tomorrow is another day, and I'll try again.

The Puzzler

There once was a girl who no one could figure out—an enigma to all, opaque as political rhetoric. But unbeknownst to everyone was the fact that she couldn't figure out anyone either. People were as mysterious to her as the existence of bumblebee knees.

One day, the girl was gifted a jigsaw puzzle. 500 pieces. She finished in an afternoon and bought three more, which were done in a day. She tried 1,000 pieces. Then 2,000. She had more rewards points with puzzlewarehouse.com than anyone in history.

She did nothing but puzzles until the day she died.

Needed Items

My friend Stella told me about this weird shop downtown. She said it had the strangest collection of books and herbs and doodads and geegaws. But the most unusual thing about the shop, according to her, was that every time she went in, she found exactly what she was needing, even though she hadn't known what that was.

So I went in, as a skeptic. No book caught my eye, no herbs spoke to me. But as I rounded a corner, I found a platter with a single chocolate éclair. From then on, I was a true believer.

Important Application

Lowry the mouse was a studious rodent. He read all the classics, practiced his long division, and knew what islands made up the Maritime provinces. He hoped to go to a good university someday.

You might wonder why a mouse would want to go to college. How short-sighted of you! Why *wouldn't* a mouse want to get a degree? Why wouldn't a mouse be curious about the world around him and want to learn more?

The biggest roadblock of course was trying to get a student loan. The "other" box on the application only got him so far.

Life Purpose

"Look," said Durga. "You're nice company and all, but how long do we have to hang around this godforsaken mountainside?"

The woman looked at her blankly. "I'd hoped you had the answer to that."

"This is *your* life, not mine, lady. So what are you going to do about it?" Durga could do this part of her job in her sleep. After battling powerful demons and having to clean up the messes of men, helping a lost woman was child's play. But she caught Crow's chastising gaze and remembered her objective. Every soul had the right to self-actualization.

First Time

When will be the ...

Last time you eat breakfast

Last time you take a walk

Last time you drive a car

Last time you take a drink of water

Last time you'll ever see the sea

Last time you put on pants

Last time you trail your fingertips in a cool stream

Last time you watch the sun set in a sky full of color

Last time you get to tell your favorite person that you love them

Last time you will take a deep breath

Do you ever wonder?

I didn't used to. But now I do.

Sensitive Creature

Ellory McFinn sat in her kitchen and watched Jack pace around the pool. The man was almost irresistible when he was deep in thought, but she wouldn't bother him while he worked.

Moments later, Jack entered the house. "Ellie, how well did you know Franklin?"

"We were lovers not long ago," she said. "I introduced him to Lesta."

Jack looked confused, then crestfallen.

"Does that surprise you?" she asked, secretly hoping to shock him, yet slightly regretful if it would ruin her chance of a future dalliance with him.

"No, but it makes you a suspect."

"Oh. Right."

Under Water

When I was little, my mom took me to the tide pools at Corona Del Mar. There was so much to see! Iridescent abalone shells, sea anemones. Fish, crabs, urchins, and starfish.

Did you know that hermit crabs outgrow their borrowed homes and must find new ones to occupy? Who were the original owners of those shells? Slow-crawling snails who have moved on to greener sea pastures.

Knowledge of the life in the sea sometimes feels as innate to me as breathing. I don't know where I learned all these things, but they'll always be part of me.

Alternate Reality

I lay on my back and sighed as I looked up at the stars. He took my hand.

"It's going to be alright," he said.

I knew it wasn't true, but it sounded nice.

I turned on my side and stretched one arm out to feel the grass with my fingers. He turned too, his body radiating warmth behind me. When he breathed, I felt the movement along my shoulder blades.

"I've got you," he said, "I'm here." One strong, kind hand rested on my hip.

We both knew it wasn't true, but it sure did sound nice.

Winter Thaw

"Look out the window," said Durga.

The woman peered out at the snowy landscape. Only now, there was no snow. The wind had stopped, and green, rolling hills had replaced the white, unforgiving mountains.

"Why have I been trying to climb so high?" she asked.

Durga sighed. "That is a question for the ages. But the short version is, humans like to make things harder than they are."

"But sometimes things really *are* hard," the woman said.

"Are they? Look. Those mountains you were climbing never end. You could keep going, but you'll never get to the top."

Love Slug

Alfred was a snail who loved everyone. Other snails, rodents, bunnies, even humans who wanted to step on him because he ate their hostas.

The animosity of others never stopped him.

Alfred loved hugs. Whether someone was jumping with joy or hopping mad, he wanted to hug them. Beings who were sad, confused, grief-stricken—he knew hugs were the answer.

No one knew how Alfred became so compassionate. Everyone said he'd always been that way, ever since he was hatched from his momma's egg.

The only problem was that Alfred had no arms with which to give hugs.

Need Want

I went to a restaurant today and a burrito and water cost me $2,000,000. I was like, *dayum*, what a bargain! I hardly eat out anymore, because all that synthetic food gives me heartburn. Plus, have you *seen* how much things cost?

And don't even get me started on clothes. I had to get a HELOC on my 1600 square-foot, $200,000,000,000 ranch house just to get a new pair of Vans.

Honestly.

Pretty soon this capitalism thing is gonna, like, blow up, and the endless grasping for corporate profits will backfire.

But first I need a new iPhone.

Seventy Plus

Kapuni Jones sat on his boat, the *Shitbucket.* It was aptly named —a dinghy the size of a Hyundai sedan with peeling paint, and a leak that had been plugged with a T-shirt belonging to his last girlfriend.

"Are you ready?" his current girlfriend called from the next slip where the *Fancy Feast,* his other boat, was moored.

Kapuni said nothing, just sighed and stood up. He wondered what she meant by *ready,* but had recently learned it was best not to ask. He really needed to date someone his own age. Or at least someone over sixty.

Heat Wave

"I'm really a suspect?" asked Ellie McFinn. She watched Detective Robinson loosen his shirt collar. The desert heat was getting to them all.

"If you and Franklin were lovers, you had a motive to kill him when you found out he'd started carrying on with Miss Runningdeer."

Ellie laughed.

Jack couldn't believe her cavalier attitude. "How can you be that way when it comes to matters of the heart?"

"Oh Jack, that's so cute. Franklin and I never had anything to do with romance. You're so naïve."

"Am I?" Jack growled, grabbing Ellie's waist and pulling her close.

Space House

Biff sat with me in the sunshine. "Did you know the top floor of my hoomans' house is detachable?" he asked.

"No way," I said.

"Oh yeah," said Biff. "At night when we're all upstairs, they close the hatch and then the man hooman pushes a button and we all go into space."

"Impressive!" I admitted. "But you blast off without a kitchen?" I could tell from Biff's expression he hadn't thought about that.

A talking dog I can deal with, but the top floor of a house that orbits the earth without snacks? I don't think so.

Old Irvine

It was a hot July day, and Alex walked her bike out of the apartment and onto the sidewalk. No one knew what "latchkey kids" were yet, but those who were one, were all too familiar with the routine. With her mom not home till dinnertime, Alex was free to roam and explore, for better or worse. No one knew, no one cared.

As the temperature rose, the dry brush gave off the scent of fire and Alex sought shade. She got off her bike and dropped into a ravine behind the complex, finding something she hadn't expected.

Come Down

She left the small shack, her clothes having dried by the fire and her body renewed by the tea that Durga had served. In the distance was a chain of snow-capped mountains, sharp and fierce. They seemed so far away now.

Under her feet was a lush carpet of meadow grass. She removed her coat, trailing it behind her until she dropped it entirely. It was time to start heading home.

If she wanted, she could head toward those mountains again, and keep trying to climb up, up, up. But for what purpose? Warmer climes suited her more.

Wind Shear

Marv wanted recognition. And not just local notoriety—world-wide fame.

He planned to spin the longest spider web ever recorded in history. According to the internet, the longest ones were three feet across.

Pish.

Marv took an Uber to Van Nuys airport. He climbed the wall of a private hanger, attached his web, and leapt onto the wing of a private jet.

That night the jet pulled out and he was on his way! The world record would be his! He'd ride that jet till it landed, attach his web to the ground, and notify the internet. Boom.

Gracious Living

In three steps, James's long legs carried him across the room and he sat down on the couch next to me.

"I've got to go," he said, and tucked a lock of my hair behind my ear.

"I know."

It was always like this. A night or two spent together, whispers of souls, promises of a future that remained a fixed distance away. Then a change in plans, then separation.

"You could come with me," he suggested as he pulled on his boots.

I smiled. I'd given those boots to him last Christmas. He'd given me my life.

Tall Tales

What do trees remember? What do they forget?

The things they've seen. And heard.

Millions of whispered confessions, millions of shouted declarations.

They've been witnesses to forbidden love.

Silently offering protection, shelter, hugs.

What do they hear when we pass by with a friend on a walk, talking about our lives? Are they judging us?

I'd like to think not.

I'd like to think they're forgiving. Patient. Understanding of the weaknesses of humans.

Do they weep as we cut them down? Are they in mourning as fires sweep through the groves?

I'd like to think they love us.

Bad Ideas

Floyd pulled his cape closed, concealing from his fellow subway riders the fact that he couldn't button his pants anymore, thanks to an unfortunate phase last year when he discovered he could order cheesecakes on the internet.

None of his pants fit, and his previous girlfriend Wanda told him once that no way should he wear sweatpants in public...So that left his cape.

A woman and her young son got on the train.

"Are you a superhero?" the boy asked Floyd.

He imagined himself to be a caped crusader. Saving people and having special powers.

"No," he said.

Wisdom Feathers

Beryl was an ornery chicken, something that had always given her great pride. But lately she felt like she'd lost her edge. She used to want to attack everyone. Now she kind of, almost, felt like getting people to pick her up so she could get some pets.

What the heck is wrong with me? she wondered.

Even that was off—she never used to use wimpy words like *heck*.

Maybe having a common-law husband and a brood of chicks had softened her. She didn't long for escape or revenge anymore.

But still, life was pretty darn great.

The After

She walked in and dropped her backpack on the floor. The house smelled strange, like it was someone else's. Who had been living here?

No one.

It just seemed different enough to not be hers anymore.

Crow hadn't come down the mountain with her and she missed him. She walked through the house and went outside, sitting in a chair on the patio. Wildflowers surrounded her—bees, butterflies too. Her shoulders released. She felt months of tension leave her body.

She looked upward and there was Crow, sitting in an elm tree. She smiled, and he flew away.

Bipedal Problems

"My feet fell off."

I was in a zoom meeting with my therapist, who raised one eyebrow at my comment. I knew that when both went up, we were onto something. Just one meant she wasn't too concerned.

"Yes, well," she said. "It's common to dream of losing appendages. Or teeth. Usually this signifies some greater sense of loss …"

"It wasn't a dream," I said. I leaned back and lifted first one leg, then the other, so she could see. "I really lost my feet. Came right off after my shower this morning."

Both eyebrows shot up.

Bark Business

"Yeah! That's it!" The director bolted out of his chair and ran toward the fake beach backdrop. "Put the dog on the surfboard!"

Arthur wagged his tail so hard that he knocked over the blond kid who'd been standing on the surfboard but was now sprawled in a pile of fake sand.

Arthur's owner Angie was skeptical. "I haven't trained him to surf yet," she said.

"I don't care! Just do it!"

Angie sighed. She really needed to talk to their agent about booking fewer commercials with coked-up directors.

But how else could a dog break into Hollywood?

Big Show

Ogden had worked at Suts Pizza for years. Everyone called it "Sucks Pizza," but it was pretty good.

Saturdays were busiest. People lined up outside for a booth. Takeout was good too, but dining in was better.

"What're those streaks on the window?" asked one woman in line who'd never been there before.

"You'll see," said her companion. "Hopefully we're not too late."

Ten minutes later, Ogden carried a large Hawaiian toward a window booth. He tripped on the edge of a floor tile, the giant pie flying into the glass, then sliding to the ground. Everyone clapped.

Home Again

Durga sat in her favorite chair at Shiva's kitchen island.

"Your mail's over there," he said, nodding to a small stack of envelopes by his espresso machine. "Where did you go, anyway?"

"Just another epic journey," said Durga. "When's that going to be ready?"

They both looked at the oven. Shiva was making his famous roasted vegetables. He smiled. "Soon."

An easy silence fell between them. Durga reflected on how nice it was to have a neighbor like Shiva. Someone who knew what her life was like and was content to just be with her.

Jai sri Durga.

Diamond Ocean

Pearl was sad. But elephant tears were so huge they could cause floods.

So she tried not to cry too much.

But Pearl was sad.

How long before she wasn't sad anymore? When a difficult situation was over, it wasn't like the stress or sadness magically went away.

Pearl didn't know what to do. Her mommy never gave her advice for things like this.

Pearl's mommy had taught her how to find tender new leaves on the tall trees, and which way to face in a rainstorm. But nothing about what to do when she felt so sad.

Aim Carefully

"This is much different than lounging by the pool," said Detective Robinson. He traced the curve of Ellory McFinn's hip with his index finger until he couldn't reach any farther, then lifted his thumb to create the shape of a gun with his hand. He shut one eye and aimed at Ellie's nose.

"You're so silly, Jack!" She laughed.

He shot her again and she grabbed his hand. "Am I still a murder suspect?" she asked.

"No."

Ellie was disappointed. "Why not?"

"Because I solved the murder earlier this afternoon. I've just been too distracted to tell you."

No Regrets

Helen poured more Chablis and pulled out three books from her twenty-volume set of photo albums, thumbing through each in turn.

Many photos were of men who looked awfully rough, but I kept quiet. I'd only moved in across the street a week ago.

Thirty minutes later, she'd brought out two more albums.

"D'ya know what you get after a lifetime of dating men who don't deserve you?"

I shrugged.

She waved her hand at the wall. "There's a world of guys out there thinking I was the best thing to ever happen to 'em. And they're right."

Hot Dang!

Throughout her life, Gladys always felt she had special powers. Just after she was born, men landed on the moon. A miracle on the heels of a miracle!

She lost a tooth on the bicentennial of Our Great Nation and that one time in 1992, on her 23rd birthday when she'd gotten a free ticket to her 23rd Grateful Dead show, she took some particularly lovely mushrooms (also free) and the band had opened with the song she'd predicted.

Now came her 50th birthday. Fluctuating hormones, menopause. Hot flashes. Which were clearly the only explanation for climate change.

Goodster Praise

Dear heatherly feather,

Blouse me in your etherlasting lurveliness. Help me sometimers see good humorless in my fallow neighslayers and also those who wash me in harmful sunrays of gloom.

Assistfulness me to underpants the bountains of fruitsy and juiciness which upends the earthly pleins surrounding my corporeal jellybag.

May I sometimes have patients with those whose varicose veined personells are upwardsing to start starwars and lie disheveledly to fronds and familiars.

Please, goodster, blast me with your abundantful benevolencing shoots so that I may waft ozonewards in golden shoes and brays of whelps and powerlessness.

Cumin,

Andrea

Best Defense

Pop Bear glared at Mom Bear. "He's *your* son," he bellowed.

Mom Bear tsked her husband. "He's most likely yours too."

They both stared at Junior Bear, who gave them a half-hearted smile.

"The fire didn't last long," he said. The look he got from his parents made him realize it was a crappy defense. "Teenagers will be teenagers?"

Mom Bear tsked him this time. "Oh, Junior."

Pop Bear crossed his arms in front of his chest. "You'd better get your ducks in a row before hibernation."

"The ducks had nothing to do with it!" cried Junior Bear.

Parts Of

The warmth of the sun on my skin after a long winter.

Holding a skein of yarn in my hands—the color and texture of possibility.

Thinking about my parents.

Wondering what someone might think if I told them I am neurodivergent.

Wondering how I'd feel after I told them.

Finishing a writing project.

Looking at my retirement accounts (on a good market day).

Watching a bird be in the moment.

Painting with watercolors with no concern for the outcome.

That first sip of coffee in the morning.

Releasing a breath I didn't even know I'd been holding.

Icy stare

Bruce shook the rain off his coat collar and steeled his jaw before entering the diner. It was dark and cold outside, but even colder inside.

He slid into the booth opposite a woman dressed in a red raincoat and matching beret. She was younger than she looked and smelled of smoke.

"You're late," she said.

Bruce said nothing, just looked at her. It was clear her features had been delicate once, but now all that remained was a coarseness produced by time and wear. He took a drink from her water glass.

All in a night's work.

Beautiful Vacay

Crow enjoyed accompanying humans on their journeys, but even he needed a break from the constant emotional flux that they were subject to. So on a crisp fall day, he informed Durga of his plans and took off.

He had no destination in mind, but north was the direction to go.

The weather cooled the farther he flew, and soon he saw no more of his kind in the skies or on the ground.

Instinct told him if he continued, he'd hit snow. So he stopped and found a tall pine tree, and settled in for a nap.

Soft Distraction

Ellie got up from the bed. It was now evening, and Detective Jack Robinson noted how her skin seemed to glow in the moonlight. She was so beautiful.

"Who killed Lesta's lover?" she asked.

In truth, he hadn't yet figured out who'd killed Franklin Whitmore. He'd questioned Lesta's household, and Lesta herself, twice. There were possibilities, but no solid lead. Ellie was still a suspect, but he hadn't been able to resist the temptation any longer.

"It's complicated," he said.

He really needed to get his head on straight and finish this investigation.

"Come back to bed, Ellie."

Frank's Place

I drove out to the Valley, not expecting to find much. No one ever found much in the Valley.

Traffic was gruesome. It took me forty minutes longer than it should've, and with the price of gas what it was, it felt like eternity.

Frank's doublewide looked empty, but if I'd learned anything, it was never to trust the looks of a doublewide.

When I got to the door, I felt for the handle of my .38 in my shoulder holster.

You never knew with Frank. He wasn't the kind of wheel you wanted to fall asleep at.

Deep Feelings

Bert came home from school and flopped onto the couch.

"Myrna, I'm in love," he said.

Myrna perched on the edge of the coffee table. "Stop calling me Myrna. I'm your mom! And you're ten. How would you know what love is?"

"Isn't it like when you can't stop thinking about someone and you just want to be with them all the time, and they feel the same? Then you do stuff together and realize they kind of bug you but maybe not all that much, so you stay together anyway?"

Damn, thought Myrna. The kid nailed it.

Slow Learners

Bean came downstairs to find Olive sitting in a patch of sunlight in the living room.

"Hey, Bean."

"Hiya, Olive."

"What's new?"

"Not much," said Bean. "I spent a little time upstairs reading about morphic resonance. Are you familiar with that?"

Olive used a back leg to scratch an itch behind her right ear. "Can't say that I am, Bean."

"Well, the general idea is that there exists a type of inherited memory. It posits that we all contribute to a collective consciousness of sorts." Bean sniffed the couch.

"Fascinating," said Olive. "It's about time humans caught up."

Garden Mutiny

The sparrows looked down at the cat they called Captain Feathers from the relative safety of their privet bush.

"Hi, guys!" said Captain Feathers.

The sparrows were silent. They knew her politeness was a rouse.

"I see they've refilled the birdfeeder. Good news, eh?" The cat grinned at them with sharp teeth and extended her claws into the soft earth. Practice.

"Not today, hussy!" said a sparrow.

"Yeah!" said another.

"We've had enough of you!"

The birds flew from bush and landed on the captain's back and head, digging in with their own tiny claws.

"Today *we* win!"

That's It

Are my best days behind me?

Our advertising-driven culture says heck no. The best is yet to come! Grey-haired people sitting in outdoor bathtubs at sunset, holding hands. Cheap cell phone service, perfect for seniors. Prescriptions for aching this-and-that, dry whatchamacallits, poorly functioning gegaws.

Lots of pills. Grandkids. Skechers.

Are my best years behind me?

I've woken up from a three-year sleep. I don't look the same, definitely don't feel the same. I'm told I don't think the same. It's an art, balancing the past and future. In a single breath, the present. Again and again.

Starting over.

Ah Ha

Detective Jack Robinson sat at the breakfast table, half-heartedly reading the morning paper and whole-heartedly admonishing himself for having slept with Ellie last night.

He wanted a relationship with her, to be with her. But he knew she wasn't the marrying kind. She was unconventional through and through.

He thought about Franklin Whitmore's murder. He needed to solve that case, so he could go home.

Ellie came downstairs and sat across from him. She smiled and didn't say a word, just took a bite out of a buttered bagel.

His eyes went wide. He knew who'd committed murder.

Big Deal

Carlotta was mad. She was so mad she was about to flip her wig. But she'd spent a lot of time fixing her wig that morning, so she opted for something else. She picked the ripest avocado from the fruit bowl and chucked it at the wall.

Not bad!

Then an apple.

Not quite.

Carlotta took the fruit bowl out to the porch, held the big dish high, and let 'er go.

Kablam!

Yes! Yes!

Next came a stack of cereal bowls.

She branched out and tried dinner plates.

Once the kitchen was bare, she felt much better.

Under Bunny

The sparrows had lost another of their ranks, courtesy of Captain Feathers.

After holding an emergency meeting, they sent an elected representative to the yard next door, to talk to the rabbits.

The rabbit family who lived in the neighbor's privet bush wasn't your average bunch of fluffy bunnies. Dad Rabbit was freakishly strong and sported extra-sharp teeth.

The sparrow explained their predicament next door and offered Dad Rabbit unlimited access to the zinnia flowerbeds all winter, if he'd help them with their "little problem."

Dad puffed up his chest and obliged. Any opportunity to play the hero.

Moon Dance

Jeff walked up to Max and handed her another beer, bobbing his head to the Chet Baker song playing in the bar. Sawdust crunched underfoot, the shuffleboard game between Sean and Dinesh was intense.

The dim, atmospheric lighting created shapes out of Sean's cigarette smoke, enthralling Max. It didn't take much alcohol before that warm, introspective, yet friendly feeling overcame her. Sean squinted through the smoke at her and smiled.

Max turned to Jeff, who was home for Thanksgiving, back to college again on Sunday. She never went anywhere.

"Want to get out of here?" she asked him.

Green Dreams

Ethel Mermaid loved her job at the One Stop Submarine Shop. Even though the seaweed snacks were hard to keep upright in their display case and she had to card everyone who bought the Something's Fishy Hard Kombucha, the job was easy and the pay was good.

One day Ethel was restocking the Siren Chips when the most beautiful mermaid she'd ever seen floated through the door. Pauletta Fishlips, teen acting sensation and star of Ethel's favorite TV show, "You've Gotta be Fishing Me." The epitome of deep-undersea glamor.

That was when Ethel decided to take acting lessons.

Same Difference

Dougie sat on the rocks overlooking St. Ninian's tombolo with his best mate, Angus.

"Had some news yesterday," said Dougie.

"Oh? What's that now?" asked Angus.

"My doctor told me I'm not 100% cormorant. Part of me is summat else."

Angus ruffled his feathers. "Interesting. So, what's it like to not be all cormorant then?"

Dougie thought about that. "What a daft question!"

"Well how're you different?"

"That's like askin' me what it's like not bein' a bird, or what it feels like to breathe air rather than water."

"You're right," said Angus. "We're all the same anyway."

Closed Case

"I'll miss Lesta," said Ellie McFinn, tossing her car keys onto the table. "I can't believe she was the one who killed poor Whitmore."

"I'm sorry I had to arrest your friend," said Detective Robinson.

"I guess this means you can go back to the city now."

Jack put his hands in his pockets. "Is that what you want?"

"I didn't say that," Ellie said.

Their eyes met.

"I know you, Ellory. You're probably ready for your next diversion."

Ellie walked up to him and ran a finger down his shirtfront. "You don't know me," she said. "Stay."

Vacation's Over

Crow landed on Durga's barbecue as she and Shiva drank beer on the patio.

"Your bird's back from vacation," said Shiva. "Must be nice, to have time off."

"If you work too hard, you've only yourself to blame," said Durga, smiling.

"I suppose."

"We could go to the beach."

Durga hoped he'd say yes. They hadn't traveled together in eons.

"Nah," said Shiva, picking at the label on his bottle. "I've got to wash my car."

Crow flew to Durga's shoulder and eyed the tiger resting at her feet. Durga sighed. The bird was right—time to go.

Special Delivery

Edith went on an afternoon walk through her neighborhood. The fall air was cool and crisp. No one was out—everyone was at work or inside on computers.

"Hey lady."

Edith looked around but didn't see anyone.

"Up here."

She looked up and a fat squirrel sat on a tree branch directly above her head.

"Did you bring the stuff?"

"Um," said Edith. She'd never encountered a talking squirrel before. Not even in college.

"Edgar said you'd bring it." The squirrel stared at her with beady eyes.

Edith stared back. "I guess I'll bring it tomorrow?"

"You better."

Grand Time

"Grampy, tell us a story!"

"I suppose I could do that. Like what?"

"What was it like when you were a kid? Was it fun?"

"Did I tell you 'bout the time I found a dead body down by the swimming hole?"

"Uh..."

"Oh! Or how about the time I ran bootleg liquor for the mob when I was twelve! I didn't have a driver's license, but no one seemed to care. Not like today."

"Uh..."

"Yessirree, it *was* fun bein' a kid. Those were the days. Bootleggin', fast cars, and loose women. And the occasional dead body."

Great State

Ellory McFinn stood on the balcony of her new home, overlooking the Pacific ocean. So much had changed since her carefree, partying days. But she was still carefree, and she did still love a party.

She'd decided to buy the desert home she'd rented for her holiday and keep it for special occasions. It was the place where she and Detective Jack Robinson had made it official, after all.

Official meaning they would be exclusive. No marriage, certainly no children. But between the dry California desert and the mist-laden coast, they would make a go of it. Together.

All Done

Barbara used to be the absolute shit. But now she was on her way out, in multiple respects. Her acting career was in the dumps since her heart attack and the three misconduct lawsuits. To prove it, here she was, filming a commercial for paper towels.

It's not like she didn't love paper towels. But how on god's green earth could you give a moving performance mopping up a spill?

After the eleventh take the director reviewed the tape and declared it a keeper.

Maybe this would be the game-changer, Barbara thought.

"That's a wrap," said the director.

Tall Tale

The family sat around the table, eating dinner.

"Someday I'm going to write a romance novel," announced Bex.

"Oh yeah?" asked Dad.

"Uh-huh. It's gonna be really mushy. Like, the main characters will have relations."

"Do you know what that word means?" asked Mom.

"Isn't that like when you kiss your cousin?" asked her little brother.

"Sorta," said Dad.

Mom looked at Bex. "What's the main conflict of your story?"

"Well, the characters are trees, and their parents don't want them to be together because one of them is an oak tree and the other is a maple."

Short Order

"Adam and Eve on a raft, and wreck 'em!" barked Wanda. She clipped an order onto the carousel standing on the counter between the kitchen and the back of the diner's bar seating.

"Unh," grunted Floyd, proprietor of Floyd's Flips, greasy spoon extraordinaire. He sometimes heard customers referring to the establishment as "Floyd's Flops," but he didn't care.

Floyd knew he was destined for greatness. Yes, he currently owned one diner on an almost-nameless highway in Arizona, and okay, it had taken him thirty years to get here. But good things were coming. They just had to be.

Ocean Bound

What if there is no heaven after we die? What if there is no hell either?

What if

All there is

Is the Love Boat.

When you die, you cross the gangplank, Captain Stubing and Gopher greet you and give you directions to your room. (Your luggage magically awaits you in your quarters, which features infinite closet space). You're on a cruise of indeterminable duration—the boat meanders at sea.

Occasionally it docks at a new location. You disembark.

When you die again, you reboard. Sometimes you get a stateroom, sometimes you get an inside room.

What if?

On Order

"Diane, are you going to the grocery store today?"

"No Jim, we have a complete food subscription now."

"Oh. Well how about we go to the mall? I need pants."

"We have a clothing subscription. Pants come next week."

"Is our coffee also by subscription?"

"Tuesdays. Same for houseplants, pet food, crayons, books, magazines, and gasoline."

"Let me guess. Do our friends get delivered on Thursdays?"

"Don't be ridiculous, Jim. You know how antisocial you are. Friends only get delivered every three months."

"Is there anything that we don't have a subscription for?"

"Hmm, let me think. Nope."

Human Tendencies

Why do I write short stories about animals? (I get accused of anthropomorphizing a lot).

Because they're easier to deal with than people.

I can tell a story about a courageous rabbit, or a gangster squirrel. Who's to tell me I'm doing it wrong?

Human emotions are tricky.

Or rather, humans are tricky!

Sometimes, I'm overly concerned with getting humans wrong. I think too much.

But in the realm of the animals, all rules can be tossed to the wayside.

What's that bird thinking? Whatever I want it to, MUAHA-HAHAHAHA!

This also goes for merpeople, Sasquatches, and trees.

What Then?

Whether I spend my time in tears from laughter or sadness, I'll end up in the same place one day. My question isn't about what lies on the other side, but more about how I'll get there.

Will I jump into the Great Abyss headfirst, and land with a sudden yet satisfying *plop*?

Will the earth tilt on its axis enough that I finally slide in, leaving claw marks in the dirt?

Do I have a choice in any of it?

I listen to the birds and watch the autumn rain, preparing for arrival yet enjoying the journey.

100/100

For Dad

I went for a walk through a field of grain; the stalks came to my shoulders and bent to the desires of a gentle breeze. Suddenly the wind intensified. I stopped in my tracks, feeling something behind me.

Durga rushed past, tall as the sky, silken robes flowing in a blur of white. I caught the look on her face. Determination like I'd never seen before.

As she moved farther away, I noticed she carried a huge scimitar with both hands.

Crow landed on the ground next to my feet.

"Fierce," I said.

"You've no idea," said Crow.

KEEP IN TOUCH

Want free stories, special discounts and ... did I mention free stories?
Sign up for the AceWrites Newsletter - a monthly email full of funness.
Visit my website at acneil.com for more info and receive a free short story.

ALSO BY ANDREA C. NEIL

THE BEVERLEY GREEN ADVENTURES

Beverley Green's First Adventure

Beverley Green's First Territorial Christmas

Beverley Green Finds True North

Beverley Green Comes Home

The Guthrie Short Stories

FLASH FICTION

Days Are Beautiful

No Surprises

Pick up a FREE short story when you subscribe to the Ace Writes
Newsletter!

For a complete list of all of Andrea's books visit her website, acneil.com
to get the full scoop.

ABOUT THE AUTHOR

Andrea is a writer, editor, and professional introvert. She balances all that with embarrassingly large servings of chocolate, peanut butter straight out of the jar, and plenty of irony. Not to be mistaken for ironing. She doesn't do any of that.

She's a Southern California native, but now calls Tulsa, Oklahoma home, where she lives with her partner and a million houseplants. Favorite pastimes include starting knitting projects, making vegetable soup, and lamenting over the existential qualities of housework.

Andrea is the niece of Eleanor and Francis Coppola, and appreciates all their inspiration and encouragement.

acneil.com

facebook.com/andreacneil

instagram.com/andreacneil

bookbub.com/authors/andrea-c-neil